BRUISED

DONNA DAVID

Bruised ISBN 978-1-78837-326-5

Text © Donna David 2018
Complete work © Badger Publishing Limited 2018

Publisher: Susan Ross
Senior Editor: Danny Pearson
Editorial Coordinator: Claire Morgan
Copyeditor: Cheryl Lanyon
Designer: Bigtop Design Ltd
Cover Illustration: Dave Robbins

2 4 6 8 10 9 7 5 3 1

CHAPTER 1
THE POSH END

Dean slung his bag over his shoulder and stepped down off the school bus. He looked around for Finn — he normally waited for him by the bus stop, but today he wasn't there.

Good, thought Dean. *I don't want to see him today anyway.*

Dean walked into his form room and threw his bag onto a chair. He sat down and put his feet up on the table. The rest of his class piled into the room.

"Where's Finn?" asked Tom.

Dean shrugged. The bell rang loudly to signal the start of school. The class fell quiet as Mrs Willis called out the register.

Dean looked over his shoulder as he heard the classroom door open. It was Finn. Late again. Dean pulled his bag off the chair to make space for him, but he wasn't going to smile. Not after Finn had left him waiting in town on Saturday for over an hour.

But Finn didn't come and sit next to Dean. He pulled a chair out right by the door, on the other side of the classroom, and sat by himself.

Just what is his problem? thought Dean.

When the bell went at the end of registration, Finn was first out of the door. Dean had to jog to catch up with him.

"Finn!" he called.

Finn kept on walking.

"Finn!" called Dean again.

Finn stopped and looked around.

"What?" he asked.

"What happened to you on Saturday? Where were you?" asked Dean.

"I was busy," answered Finn. He looked tired. There were dark circles under his eyes and his hair needed a wash.

"Too busy to answer your phone?" asked Dean. Dean had rung him twenty times. He'd left a voicemail and sent messages, but Finn had just ignored them all.

"I said — I was busy!" snapped Finn. "I was packing my stuff up — I've moved in with my gran."

"What?" said Dean. "Your gran that lives down by the canal?"

Finn looked down at the ground. He shifted from side to side.

"Yeah," he said, quietly. "She lives by the canal."

Dean whistled. "Nice!" he laughed. "You've moved to the posh end of town. Don't forget me now you're living with the millionaires!"

Finn barely smiled.

"My dad did some work over there last year," said Dean, "and he said that they all have swimming pools."

Dean was enjoying imagining Finn's new house. He could picture the swimming pool, the pool room, the gaming room. He bet Finn's gran would have a fully-stocked fridge all day, every day.

"So, when can we come over?" asked Dean.

Finn looked up quickly. "What?"

"When are you asking us all over?" Dean insisted. "House-warming party, right? We can get everyone round."

Finn frowned, but didn't answer.

"Or I'll just come on my own," Dean tried again. "We can raid your gran's fridge and watch TV. I bet your gran goes to bed at nine."

Finn shook his head. "Just give it a rest, Dean. You're not invited, OK?"

Finn turned his back on Dean and walked off towards the maths block.

Just what is his problem? thought Dean for the second time that morning. Dean was the one who'd been left hanging around town like a total loser, and yet it was Finn who was storming off in a mood.

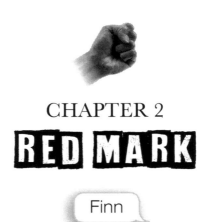

CHAPTER 2
RED MARK

Finn

Finn kicked at a stone as he walked past the biggest houses he'd ever seen. There was a man pulling up weeds in the front garden of one of them. Finn bet that he didn't live there. People who lived in houses like that didn't weed their own gardens. They had gardeners for that sort of thing.

Finn walked past the final garden in the row and cut down the alley that ran down the side of the huge house. When he came out the other side he was on the canal.

He pulled his phone out of his pocket and frowned. He had no reception here. Finn would never get why Gran had chosen to live on a shabby houseboat right behind the poshest houses in town. The lads at school would rip it out of him if they knew he was living on an old, busted canal boat.

Finn shoved his phone back in his pocket. No reception and no Wi-Fi. Great. How was he supposed to know if his mum was trying to get in touch? She might need him and he'd be stuck out here.

Well if she needs me, it will serve her right for kicking me out, thought Finn. But even as he thought it, Finn knew that it wasn't true. It wasn't his mum who had kicked him out. It was Mark.

Mark was his mum's new boyfriend and he hated Finn. Finn didn't care because he hated Mark too.

Mark had been alright when Finn had first met him. He'd taken Finn and his mum to the cinema a few times and he always treated them to a burger afterwards. But once he'd moved in, everything had changed.

Mark would walk around the house in nothing but a pair of stained tracksuit bottoms. He'd lie on the sofa watching daytime TV whilst Finn's mum rushed around cleaning, tidying and cooking. All before she had to leave to work her shift at the care home.

Finn hated watching his mum getting ordered around by Mark, but then things got worse. Mark decided that Finn was lazy. He told Finn's mum that Finn was taking advantage, that he wasn't pulling his weight. He said that Finn was taking all their food and running up their bills and not helping with anything. Finn was quick to point out that it wasn't Mark's food and Mark wasn't paying any of the bills, and that's when Mark hit him.

Finn held his bruised ribs as he thought back to the blazing row he'd had with Mark on Saturday.

The one that had ended with his mum crying and Mark yelling and Finn getting kicked out onto the street.

Finn had spent that evening just walking around. He'd sat in the bus shelter for a couple of hours, checking his phone every few minutes in case his mum had texted. Eventually she did. She asked Finn to meet her at the end of the road.

Finn had smiled when he read the message. Finally his mum was leaving Mark. Finally they could go back to how things had been before.

Finn had burned with anger when he saw the red mark on his mum's face.

"It's nothing, love," she said, as she gave him a hug.

Then she handed him a plastic bag. Confused, Finn opened the bag and looked inside. Clothes. A bag full of Finn's clothes with his toothbrush on top.

"Go to Gran's," she said. "She's got a spare bed."

Finn took the bag, too shocked to speak. His mum hugged him tightly one last time and then turned and ran back to the house. It was then that Finn noticed that she was still wearing her slippers.

"Don't go back," called Finn, but she was already too far away to hear.

That was why Finn hadn't turned up to meet Dean that evening, and now Dean was sulking about it.

He's got no idea what things are like for me, thought Finn.

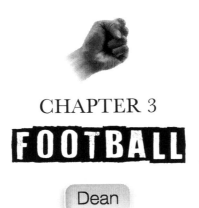

CHAPTER 3

FOOTBALL

Dean

Dean flicked through his phone as he waited for his game to load.

Still nothing from Finn.

Ever since Finn had moved to the other side of town he had stopped replying to Dean's messages. It was like he thought he was too good for Dean now. He wouldn't even game with him anymore.

The game was finally loaded. Dean checked to see who was online. Betablast, LittleLizard and SaturnX were all there, but no BitBoy.

BitBoy was Finn's gamer tag and this was the sixth night in a row that he hadn't logged on.

He's probably joined some other game, thought Dean as he threw his controller onto his bed.

Finn had been acting strangely at school all week. He'd forgotten his homework in French, which was pretty standard for Finn, but he'd also forgotten his PE kit. Finn never forgot his PE kit. He was one of the best footballers in the school and if he wasn't gaming, then he'd be kicking a football about.

But this week things had been different. Mr Greg had said that Finn could borrow a kit, but Finn refused. The kit from lost property was pretty gross, but Dean would have thought that playing football in a mouldy old kit was better than not playing any football at all.

Finn would have agreed two weeks ago. Before he moved in with his gran. Before he thought he was too good for his old friends.

Then Finn hadn't joined in with their football match at break time either. They were only messing about on the field. He didn't really even have to run. Just pass it to Dean or one of the other lads.

"Come on, Finn," Dean had said. "Get up and pass the ball."

"Nah," Finn had replied. "I'm alright down here."

Finn was lying down on the grass and wasn't showing any signs of getting up. Miss Malone, the school counsellor, was on duty.

"Not joining in today, Finn?" she asked.

Finn shook his head.

"He's given up on football, Miss," said Dean.

"Is everything alright, Finn?" asked Miss Malone.

Finn mumbled something about everything being fine and he turned away.

Dean watched Miss Malone stand there for a few moments. He watched as she looked at Finn's shirt. It was kind of grubby. There was a food stain on it that had been there since last week. Finn had rolled up his sleeves and Dean could see some old, blue bruises, almost faded. Miss Malone could see them too.

Dean jogged over. "You going to join in or what?" he asked.

Finn got to his feet.

"No, I'm not," said Finn. "I'm too tired."

"Were you gaming all night?" asked Dean, trying to keep his voice steady.

"Yeah," laughed Finn briefly. "That's the best thing about living with my gran — she goes to bed way before me. I was online until two in the morning!"

Dean shook his head.

"I tried finding you online to invite you to my game last night," he said.

Finn shrugged. "I was busy."

"I guessed," answered Dean bitterly. He turned around and booted the football across the field. Then he ran after it, leaving Finn standing on his own.

Finn turned around and walked back towards the school, shoulders slumped.

Miss Malone watched him walk away.

CHAPTER 4
BLOOD

Finn

"You coming out tonight?" called Dean as Finn queued up to get on the school bus.

"No," said Finn. "I've got plans."

Dean turned and walked away. "Of course you have," he muttered under his breath.

Finn found a seat at the back of the bus and sat down. He sat nearest the aisle so that no one could sit down next to him.

He'd sent his mum three text messages earlier in the day and she hadn't replied to any of them. Finn found 'Mum' in his list of contacts and called her. He listened as the phone rang and rang before going to answerphone. He tried again. The same thing happened. When Finn tried again a third time, the phone went straight to answerphone.

When Finn got off the bus fifteen minutes later, he had made up his mind. He was going to see his mum. He needed some clean clothes and his PE kit. His gran's washing machine still needed fixing and he didn't want to walk around in dirty clothes anymore.

Maybe Mark will be out, thought Finn, but he knew that was wishful thinking.

Finn walked down his street. When he got to his house, his heart started thundering in his chest. He took a deep breath, pushed open the low, chipped gate and walked up the path. He knocked on the door and waited.

He could hear the TV blasting from the front room and he knew that meant that Mark must be home.

Finn lifted his hand and knocked again, louder this time.

The volume of the TV was turned down and, through the glass windows in the front door, Finn could see movement. The person moving was too big to be his mum.

Mark.

Finn took a step back from the front door as Mark pulled it open.

"What do you want?" snapped Mark.

Mark was wearing his stained tracksuit bottoms. He looked like he hadn't had a shower in a few days. He took a long swig from a can of lager.

"I said… what do you want?"

"I'm just here to see Mum," answered Finn.

"Your mum's not here," said Mark, taking another swig. He finished what was left and crushed the can in his hands. He threw the empty can at Finn's feet.

Finn took a step backwards. "When will she be back?" he asked.

"None of your business," said Mark. "Your mum doesn't want to see you. You don't live here anymore."

Finn looked at Mark and his lips curled up in disgust. How dare he stop him from seeing his mum. She would never say she didn't want to see him anymore. Would she?

"Look, can I just get my stuff? I need some more things for school."

"This isn't your house," snarled Mark. "If you take anything from here then I'll have you arrested for theft. Get it?"

"I just want my stuff," said Finn. His voice was getting louder now.

Mark turned and looked indoors. Straight away Finn was suspicious.

"What are you looking at?" said Finn. "Is Mum in there?"

"Just go away," said Mark. He tried to shut the front door, but Finn put his foot in the way.

"Mum!" yelled Finn. "Mum, are you in there?"

"I said go away!" shouted Mark. He stepped out of the house and gave Finn a hard shove. Finn staggered back and fell onto the path. He quickly scrambled to his feet. Anger pulsed through his body.

Mark laughed.

What happened next was almost a blur. Finn, burning with rage, ran at Mark. He'd meant to shove him out of the way. He'd meant to get into the house to see if his mum was there, to see if she was OK, but Mark was ready. He'd been expecting it and, as Finn ran at him, Mark raised his fist and smashed it into Finn's face. Finn heard a sickening crunch as Mark's fist smacked into his nose. For the second time, Finn staggered back and fell to the ground. This time he wasn't getting up in a hurry.

Finn's head was pounding and a warm trickle of blood ran out of his nose and into his mouth. Finn spat onto the ground and looked at the blood on the path in front of him. His eyes burned with tears but he refused to cry in front of Mark.

"Your mum doesn't want to see you," snarled Mark again. He slammed the front door shut, leaving Finn on the ground.

Still on his hands and knees, Finn crawled off the path onto the patchy grass of the front garden. He thumped the ground hard. Once. Twice. Three times. Again and again he pounded the ground until his throbbing knuckles forced him to stop.

He looked back up at the house. Mark's house now. There was no sign of movement from inside and the TV was at full volume once more.

Finn dragged himself to his feet and staggered down the path. When his phone beeped he snatched it out of his pocket.

Mum?

It was Dean.

See you online tonight? If you're not too busy with your new life?

Finn stuffed his phone back into his pocket.

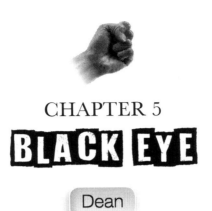

CHAPTER 5

BLACK EYE

Dean

That was it! Dean was fed up. If Finn couldn't be bothered to return his calls or answer his messages, then Dean wasn't going to bother with him anymore. He would hang out with people who actually liked having him around.

When Dean walked into registration on Monday morning, Finn wasn't there. He wasn't there during first lesson or second lesson either.

Dean pretended not to care.

It wasn't until break time that Finn finally made an appearance. He walked onto the school field where Dean and the rest of the lads were playing football.

"Whoa! What happened to you?" cried Tom. The football bounced across the grass, but everyone was looking at Finn. Dean had planned on ignoring Finn. He was going to go back inside to get a drink, but when he looked up and saw Finn, he changed his mind.

Finn had a huge black eye. The bruise was blue and purple and Finn's whole face looked swollen. There was a small cut on Finn's nose.

Finn put his hand up to his face and managed a laugh.

"I was at a party Saturday night," he said. "It all kicked off and the police were called."

Everyone was listening now.

"The police knocked down the door and we all ran for it!"

"Cool!" laughed Tom. "Where was the party?"

Finn stumbled for a moment. "Oh, just some girl who lives by my gran."

"But how did you get the black eye?" asked Tom.

"One of the police officers," said Finn. "He tried to take me down. He got me pretty good." Finn touched his bruised eye gently. "But I was too fast."

"Awesome," said Tom. He booted the football across the field and the game was back on.

Before running after the ball, Tom punched Finn playfully in the arm. Dean couldn't be sure, but it looked like Finn winced.

"You joining in?" asked Dean.

"Huh?" answered Finn. He'd been miles away. "Oh, sure," he said.

For the rest of break the boys kicked the ball around, but Dean couldn't be bothered anymore. He dropped out to the side and lay down on the field. He plucked blades of grass and watched Finn.

Finn wasn't concentrating. He wasn't running for the ball and he wasn't tackling anyone. He only noticed that the ball was anywhere near him if someone yelled his name.

Miss Malone walked up to Dean. She crouched down next to him and watched the game in silence for a minute or so.

"How is everything?" she eventually asked.

"Good," lied Dean. He didn't take his eyes off Finn.

"And Finn?" asked Miss Malone.

Dean looked at her. She looked straight at Dean, frowning slightly.

"How's Finn doing?" she asked again.

"He's a bit bruised," said Dean. He laughed unconvincingly.

"He is, isn't he?" said Miss Malone. She didn't laugh. She didn't even smile.

"You know," she continued, "you can talk to me about anything. I can take you out of lessons and we can chat any time."

Dean nodded his head. He didn't need to talk to the school counsellor.

"If you've got any worries you can talk to me," said Miss Malone. "Or if you're worried about a friend…" Miss Malone let her last sentence hang there for a few seconds.

The sound of the school bell made them both jump. Break time was over. Miss Malone stood up.

"You can call in to my office any time, Dean," she said.

Dean hauled himself to his feet. The footballers ran over to join him as they made their way back into school. Dean looked around, but Finn wasn't there.

And when Dean took his seat in maths a few minutes later, Finn's seat remained empty.

Dean got up and walked out of the classroom before the teacher arrived.

CHAPTER 6

TOGETHER

Finn

Finn hadn't bothered going back into school with the others when the bell went. He'd wandered to the edge of the field and sat down amongst the trees.

He got his phone out and dialled his mum's number. Now there was just a strange beeping sound. Finn lay down in the grass and covered his face with his hands. His eye was throbbing. He'd had a headache all weekend and it hurt to breathe out of his nose. His gran was mad at him because she thought he'd been fighting and neither of them could get in touch with his mum.

Finn felt a shadow over his face and squinted up at the figure standing above him.

Dean.

"You alright?" said Dean.

"Yeah," answered Finn. He sat up in the grass, flinching slightly as the sudden movement made his head spin.

"You're not," said Dean. "You're not alright."

Finn looked at his best friend. He'd grown up with Dean. They'd had their first fight over a tricycle at nursery and they'd been pretty much inseparable ever since.

"It's Mark, isn't it?" said Dean.

Finn nodded. He didn't trust himself to speak, but he needed to tell someone. Finn took a few deep breaths and Dean sat down beside him. In his own time, Finn told Dean everything. He told Dean about Mark and the punches. He told

Dean about being kicked out and having to live with his gran on the boat. He told Dean about having no Wi-Fi and not being able to get in touch with his mum.

"I haven't spoken to her in a week," said Finn. "I just want to know she's OK."

Dean stood up and pulled Finn to his feet.

"Come on," he said. "Let's go."

"Where are we going?" asked Finn.

"To find your mum."

"Now?"

"Yes, now," said Dean.

*

Half an hour later, Dean and Finn got off the bus at the end of Finn's road. They were almost there.

"You know, I was talking to Miss Malone today," said Dean.

"Yeah?" said Finn.

"She said we can talk to her anytime. I can. Or you can. Or we can go together."

"Yeah?" asked Finn.

"Yeah," Dean said with a smile.

"That might be alright," said Finn.

"We can go to her office tomorrow, if you like?" said Dean. "It will get us out of French!"

Finn laughed. "OK."

The two stopped talking as they reached Finn's house. Finn slowed down so that he had almost stopped, so Dean pushed open the garden gate. Finn followed behind him. Dean made sure he could feel his mobile phone in his pocket. He was ready to call the police if things got nasty again.

Dean lifted his arm to knock on the door, but before he had the chance, the door swung open.

"Mum!" cried Finn.

"Finn!"

Dean quietly moved out of the way as Finn's mum half-ran, half-stumbled out of the house and threw her arms around Finn.

For a moment neither of them spoke and Dean turned away to give them a bit of time. Then Finn gently pulled away from his mum. He looked a bit embarrassed, but mostly happy.

"I was just on my way to school," she said. "They rang and said you'd gone missing. I would have called but I couldn't remember your number and my mobile phone isn't working. Mark smashed it. Dean — you'd better give your mum a ring too."

Dean snatched his phone out of his pocket. He had six missed calls from his mum — she was not going to be happy!

Dean walked down the path to call Miss Malone. His mum was going to be so mad! Maybe Miss Malone could calm her down first. Finn was left with his mum.

"I'm so, so, sorry," said his mum, her eyes swimming with tears. "I should have kicked him out months ago."

"He's gone?" asked Finn.

Finn's mum smiled sadly. "He's gone. Laura from next door told me what happened. She told me what Mark did to you." His mum gently put her fingers on Finn's bruised face. "Laura helped me. Helped me to see that Mark wasn't right. That THIS wasn't right. Together, we called the police." She was shaking. "They came and arrested him. I'm so sorry, Finn," she repeated.

Finn shrugged his shoulders and smiled. "It's OK."

"It's not," said his mum fiercely. Then she added in a gentler voice, "But I'll make it up to you. I promise."

Finn gave her another quick hug just as Dean finished his phone call.

"I just spoke to Miss Malone. She's sorted it with the school." Dean smiled. "And she's going to sort it with my mum as well!"

Finn laughed.

"She said she'll see us tomorrow," added Dean. "During French, yeah?"

"Yeah," said Finn.

Finn's mum smiled at them both.

"So, you're not in any trouble?" she asked.

"I don't think so," said Finn. "Not any more. We're going to be alright, Mum, both of us."

THE END

Helplines and Websites relating to Domestic Violence

Childline: www.childline.org.uk

If you're under 18 you can confidentially call, email or chat online about any problem big or small.

Freephone 24-Hour Helpline: 0800 1111

Refuge: www.refuge.org.uk

Freephone 24-Hour National Domestic Violence Helpline:

0808 2000 247 (Run in partnership between Women's Aid and Refuge)

Barnardo's: www.barnardos.org.uk

Barnardo's provides a range of services to children, young people and families across the UK, addressing problems including domestic violence.